TWINKLE TWINKLE

ILLUSTRATED BY MORGAN HUFF

TWINKLE TWINKLE

LITTLE STAR

UP ABOVE THE WORLD

IN THE SKY

TWINKLE TWINKLE

LITTLE STAR

HOW I WONDER
WHAT YOU ARE

TWINKLE TWINKLE

read together, sing together

ILLUSTRATED BY MORGAN HUFF

Book design by Kris Dresen and Veronica Wagner

Copyright © 2018 Phoenix International Publications, Inc. All rights reserved.

8501 West Higgins Road, Chicago, Illinois 60631

Published by Phoenix International Publications, Inc.

p i kids and *we make books come alive* are trademark of Phoenix International Publications, Inc. and are registered in the United States.

Paperback edition published in 2022 by Crabtree Publishing Company
ISBN 978-1-6499-6650-6 Printed in China

Customer Service: orders@crabtreebooks.com

Crabtree Classroom
A division of Crabtree Publishing Company
347 Fifth Avenue, Suite 1402-145
New York, NY, 10016

Crabtree Classroom
A division of Crabtree Publishing Company
616 Welland Ave.
St. Catharines, ON, L2M 5V6

This version is available
through Crabtree Classroom

Crabtree Classroom
crabtreebooks.com